Syd Hoff
Danny and the Dinosaur Go to Camp
Hoff, Syd
Fiction
1.8

DEMCO

DANNY and the DINOSAUR Go to Camp

story and pictures by
SYD HOFF

HarperCollins*Publishers*

HarperCollins®, 🏠®, and I Can Read Book®
are trademarks of HarperCollins Publishers Inc.

Danny and the Dinosaur Go to Camp
Copyright © 1996 by Syd Hoff
Printed in the U.S.A. All rights reserved.

Library of Congress Cataloging-in-Publication Data
Hoff, Syd, date
    Danny and the dinosaur go to camp / story and pictures by Syd Hoff.
        p.   cm. — (An I can read book)
    Summary: Danny and his friend the dinosaur go to summer camp together.
    ISBN 0-06-026439-X. — ISBN 0-06-026440-3 (lib. bdg.)
    [1. Dinosaurs—Fiction.   2. Camps—Fiction.]   I. Title.   II. Series.
PZ7.H672Dap   1996   95-12410
                                                              CIP
                                                              AC

1   2   3   4   5   6   7   8   9   10
❖
First Edition

For Sally

Danny went to camp

for the summer.

He took along his friend

the dinosaur.

5

"Camp is fun.

You will enjoy it," said Danny.

"Thanks. I needed a vacation,"

said the dinosaur.

6

"Welcome," said the camp owner.

"You're the first dinosaur

we ever had here."

Lana the leader said,

"Let's start with a race.

On your mark, get set, go!"

The dinosaur took a step.

"You win!" shouted Danny.

9

The children played football.

The dinosaur ran with the ball,

and nobody could stop him.

"Touchdown!" shouted Danny.

11

Lana took everybody to the lake.

"Here is where we row our boats,"

she said.

The children rowed little boats.

Danny rowed the dinosaur.

It was time for lunch.

"Please pass the ketchup,"

said Danny.

14

"Of course, just as soon as

I finish this bottle,"

said the dinosaur.

After lunch

everybody wrote letters home.

"Please send me my own ketchup,"

Danny wrote.

16

"Send me a pizza,"

wrote the dinosaur.

17

"Now let's go on a hike,"

said Lana,

18

and everybody followed her.

Then Danny got tired

and climbed on the dinosaur.

20

"Wait for us!

We're tired too!"

shouted the children.

"Hold tight," said the dinosaur.

The dinosaur even carried Lana!

It got dark.

Everybody sat around the campfire.

Lana gave out toasted marshmallows.

"Here, have all you want,"

she said.

"Thanks, but I don't have room

for more," said Danny.

26

"I have room,"

said the dinosaur.

It was time for bed.

"I can't wait to get

under the covers,"

said Danny.

28

"Me too," said the dinosaur.

But the dinosaur's bunk

was too small for him.

He took a pillow

and went outside.

"Wake me up for breakfast,"

said the dinosaur,

and he fell asleep on the ground.

"Good night," Danny said.

32